Little Chick's
Big Day

Weekly Reader Books Presents

Little Chick's Big Day

Mary DeBall Kwitz

Pictures by Bruce Degen

An Early I CAN READ Book®

Harper & Row, Publishers

This book is a presentation of Weekly Reader Books.
Weekly Reader Books offers book clubs for children from
preschool through high school. For further information write to:
Weekly Reader Books, 4343 Equity Drive, Columbus, Ohio 43228.

Published by arrangement with Harper & Row, Publishers, Inc.
Weekly Reader is a trademark of Field Publications.
I Can Read Book is a registered trademark of
Harper & Row, Publishers, Inc.

Library of Congress Cataloging in Publication Data
Kwitz, Mary DeBall.
    Little Chick's Big Day.

    (An Early I can read book)
    SUMMARY: Little Chick ventures away from her mother
and discovers the wonders of the world beyond home.
    [1. Chickens—Fiction]   I. Degen, Bruce.
II. Title.
PZ7.K976Lf 1981   [E]   80-7905
ISBN 0-06-023667-1
ISBN 0-06-023668-X (lib. bdg.)

For Bill and Suzanne

"Come, Little Chick,"

clucked Broody Hen.

"Crawl under my wing.

It is time for your nap."

"No!" yelled Little Chick.

She ran and hid

in the garden.

"I am too big for naps,"

she whispered

to a string bean.

8

Broody Hen came
into the garden.
"Come, Little Chick,"
she clucked.

Little Chick ran and hid
in the barn.
The cow was chewing her cud.
Her calf was taking a nap
in the straw.
"I am too big for naps,"
Little Chick whispered
to the calf.

Broody Hen came

into the barn.

"Come, Little Chick,"

she clucked.

"No!" yelled Little Chick.

She ran out the barn door.

She ran and ran.

She ran past the tractor.

She ran through the tall grass.

She ran all the way

to the pond.

Little Chick had never come
this far before.

She could not see the barn.

She could not see Broody Hen.

She was all alone.

She sat down by the pond.

The sun felt warm
on her feathers.

She watched a dragonfly

zigzag

through the sunshine.

She watched a butterfly

sip

from a morning glory.

Little Chick sat very still.

"I like it here," she said.

She heard a bee buzz

in the tall grass.

She heard a frog croak

in the pond.

She looked down into the water.

A little chick, just like herself,

looked up at her.

Little Chick asked,

"Are you too big for naps, too?"

The little chick in the water

did not say anything.

Little Chick did not care.

She looked at the pond

shining in the sun

and she was happy.

Then she remembered Broody Hen.

Little Chick waited and waited.

But she did not hear

Broody Hen clucking.

She did not hear her say,

"Come, Little Chick."

Little Chick thought,

"Maybe Broody Hen cannot find me."

Then she thought,

"Maybe I am lost."

21

Little Chick looked all around.

Where was the barn?

She saw the tall grass

blowing in the wind.

But she could not see the barn.

She could not see Broody Hen.

Little Chick looked down

at the little chick in the water.

"Are you lost?" she asked.

The little chick in the water

did not say anything.

23

Little Chick said,

"I am not lost.

I will find my Broody Hen."

Little Chick ran back

through the tall grass.

"BROODY HEN!" she called.

She saw the tractor.

She ran around the tractor,

and there was the barn.

"I am home!" cried Little Chick.

She ran into the barn.

The cow was chewing her cud.

Her calf was having lunch.

But where was Broody Hen?

Little Chick ran to the barnyard.

There sat Broody Hen.

She was taking a dust bath.

"Broody Hen!" yelled Little Chick.

"Where were you?"

"I was right here,"

said Broody Hen.

"I was waiting for

my Little Chick."

"I went to the pond,"

said Little Chick.

28

"I know," said Broody Hen.

"I saw you go to the pond.

But I knew you would come home.

You are my big Little Chick."

Broody Hen went to a shady place

next to the barn.

She sat down and fluffed out
her feathers.

Little Chick crawled under her wing.

"I am glad I am not lost,"
Little Chick said.

"I am glad, too," said Broody Hen.

Broody Hen closed her eyes
and clucked a sleepy song.

Little Chick peeped out

at the barnyard.

"Tomorrow," Little Chick whispered,

"I will go to the pond again."